DIARY OF A TRADEMARK

Craig

love & bless
r Peterborough

J x

Cover design by David Campbell.
Cover photo of Ian Stephens by Melissa Auf Der Mar
Photo on flap by TSHI

Acknowledgments:
Queeries, Montreal Mirror, Oralpalooza, Sounds New, Salut les riches, Red she Said, Xero Magazine.

Thanks to Alx Espinosa, family, friends, Nini, for support at every level; also doctors and nurses, kind strangers at the Chest, Vic, General, on the streets, at the London Zoo, without whom I'm not sure I'd bother. . . .

Also Endre Farkas, poet/publisher, who has the courage to publish against the grain, David Campbell, Will Aiken and Darius James, Tshi, Melissa Auf Der Mar, Lynn Suderman, Tammy, CKUT, Tony, Paul, Joyce, Glenda, Michael, Kevin Komoda, Michael Williams, Pheobe Greenberg, Puelo Deir, Ava Chisling, Peter Scowan, Joy Gilden, Al & Shelly, Joe Clark, Lilly Peter, Jill Battson, Fortner Anderson, *L'Androgyne, Lil' Buck* and all musicians with whom I had the pleasure to jam.

Names and some of the incidents have been changed to protect the absurd.

Published with the assistance of the Canada Council and Le Ministère de la Culture.

Printed and bound in Canada by Imprimere D'éditions Marquis Ltée.

Dépôt légal, Bibliothèque Nationale du Québec and the National Library of Canada, 4th trimester, 1994

Canadian Cataloguing in Publication Data

Stephens, Ian, 1954—
    Diary of a Trademark
Poems.
ISBN 0-919754-51-1
    I. Title.
PS8587.T4653D43 1994   C811'.54   C94-900518-5
PR9199.3.S84D43 1994

The Muses' Company
P.O. Box 214
Ste. Anne de Bellevue
Québec, Canada
H9X 3R9

For information in Ian Stephens' CD
—Wining Dining Drilling—
contact EnGuard Records 2230 Coursel St.
Montreal, Quebec,
Canada, H39 1C5

DIARY OF A TRADEMARK

IAN STEPHENS

The Muses' Company

Table of Contents

". . . I'm under contract, I'm underground, know all the dirt, the Melrose sound, worked porn, reborn, sushi tongue, don't scream, I'm the knife on the beach, the golden boy, the beak that falls, cut taco meat, vd creep, I'm an actor, bad writer, a psycho-painter, a model, a dick, a cigarette butt, a rubber snake, I'm a busboy, I'm yr busboy. . . ."
— Ecstasy, LA '86

Weary State of Grace

Eight days after I was released from the hospital I was eating a hotdog near where I live in St. Henri. My first dog in months, smothered in chartreuse sauce and catsup. And a remarkably *Orange Crush* in a plastic cup and fries that oozed/glowed like slag in the rain. Yum Yum. The world worships food; wining, dining, digesting, defecating. Yum Yum Yum. When I was ill I found it grotesque, surreal, absurd – existence is consumption – an endless river, oceans of piss & shit, mouths & holes, from Somalia to the Ritz.

Since early fall I'd had pain crawling in my own gut. I suffered diarrheic streams, bogs and black vomit for several months. Despite the knowledge of my HIV+ status – my T-4 cell level being relatively high – I could only theorize about what was making me sick. I didn't think it related to my immune status, neither did my doctor. Over a period of months he arranged tests: sonar, a gastroscopy (g-scope), biopsies and x-rays at the Victoria Hospital.

Nailed and twisted by the pain, by Christmas I couldn't write, dance the fandango or eat. I had lost around twenty pounds so I went to a specialist at the General. He was businesslike but not unsympathetic. Less than a week later he told me that they had spotted something on the x-ray, enough to warrant a colonoscopy (c-scope). They put a camera and lighting crew up my butt on the end of a snake-like apparatus and found a throbbing orange and purple tumour, a cancerous obstruction between distended bowels. I could see it on a screen over my shoulder. Lymphoma! Lympho*mania!!* It looked shy, an innocent ragfish caught in the glare of publicity with a mouthful of my gut in his gristled maw.... Recent studies indicate that lymphoma is inspired by the HIV virus – they've been photographed dancing in the dark by the river.

Half an hour later, I'm in a wheelchair. I see myself in a reflection in the elevator's doors; a spidery guy with a plastic identification bracelet, ragfish and a room number....

My folding bed overlooks a cold grey Montreal. I leave messages on phone machines, put on a crisp hospital gown and get a weekly rate on a tv. A nice nurse talks about the latest in surgical hosiery - it's Clot Prevention week - but I'm drifting. All I know is that they were taking the garbage out of my torso.

The multitude of tests began. I get pushed around by strangers up and down the floors. I become a stranger and student of my body. Doctors drop by for quick chats; immuniologists, hematologists, oncologists, surgeons, an aids doctor, nutritionists, dentists; lots of strategies, sober stories, maps weighed. I slept through the twirling cheerleaders....

One day the surgeon appears beside me. She smiles and outlines the procedure which involves a shave, drugs and a cut, a slice from solar plexus to above my cock, a blade through the muscle, removing the lymphomoid growth, the obstructive tumour, and reattaching the healthy remaining ends of my bowels together. *Et Voilà!* I think it's great. I cheer, I clap my paws; it's *Wunderbar!* I sign a form and vomit a cup of tea into a bedpan. Yipee!!

I won't swallow as much for six days.

That night I sleep but the ragfish is gnawing into my groin. A nurse asks me if I need anything. I turn on my side towards the curtain lowering the elastic on my pajamas, a needle sinks into my hip, *Demerol* washes through me and the pain drains from my body. I feel a rush and my head is thrown back.

Someone inside me wants me to feel guilty for being stoned, I try to explain - hospitals were built for this, legal mercy.

Nurses understand. I had only one unfortunate experience with legal mercy - the night before surgery a novice tries to put an IV into my hand. It's not easy. She has a brittle determined look as she digs again and again for a vein. I ask her to forget it, give me some benzos but she has to try three times. A regulation, she says.

10

That's ridiculous, I pull my arm away. I want more *Demerol*. She says not for another three hours. I stare at the tv, I refuse to let her near my arm. She departs; infomercials; a man throwing money into the air, a Californian, big white teeth. I should believe in him, he says. I do believe, I say, I believe every fuking word. Jerk.

At two-thirty, the pain is too much – I stop Karla in the hall. She checks the chart, I roll up my sleeve by the nurse's station.

Later that morning, delivered to the abbatoir, the surgeons cut me open.

After the two hour surgery, another couple of hours in the recovery room, they dump my body back into the bed on the roof of the World Trade Centre – everything vague, voices and silhouettes mingle with strangers, fever, traffic, wind and delirium.

My temperature fluctuates for two days. I have pneumonia in my lungs. The drug specialist with a dashing Cyrano de Bergerac beard chooses a yellow antibiotic for me to suck through the IV along with the morphine that I control through a seven-minute pain-machine.

At this point, I am basically a wreck, emaciated by the pre-surgery fast, the tests, the lyphoma; I'm haunted by the pain they say I do not feel; the loss of blood, pneumonia.

The surgeon tells me everything went well. I look at her; her open face, her beautiful skin. I believe her. In a haze, hour by hour, I begin to recover.

Yet everything has changed. I've been split, broken, bled: I'm half-dead. Rubber gloves have been inside me, sloshing around in the bucket. My face is gaunt. My voice is other-worldly, strained and hollow; I sound like somebody else and talk about potatoes. I have a catheter on my dick, fifteen staples and foot-long scar on my tummy.

I'm alive and haunted by rubber gloves tenderly touching me, piercing my limbs with needles.

11

I hear the snowplows. It's been a horrible winter. I sit up and watch the black river and the white luminescent wing of Mt. Bruno electrified for night-skiers.

Noises, voices echo through me. The Moaning Mantra of Death from Doris, a patient in the next room – "God is pain, where is Al? God is pain, where is Al?" Someone crying, a rattle from the lungs. One night there's a stampede down the hall, a broken heart, nurses, doctors, code 99, the trolley and the IV balloons shaking.

A turquoise hyacinth exudes a rich perfume in my corner. Batches of pink azalea arrive from distant family, sit on the radiator with carnations, roses, a grey telegram from Peter, Paul and Mars.

I also miss those who don't care, past intimates who made promises when I told them I was +.... It's not their fault, they just don't know what to do.

I don't either....

I shuffle down the floor with my buddy, Mr. IV. I visit other patients across the hall as they sleep. I stare out the window – the mountain trees, boney gray branches – I ask them what I should do. They don't know either and they're in worse shape than me.

For days I am not permitted food or drink; I suck what I can from an aquamarine sponge-stick. A friend spreads vaseline over my cracked lips. I kiss her fingers. *Les becs douces.* I spend most hours with half-open eyes, doing drugs, wasted and sore.

Meanwhile, my temperature is high. The pneumonia persists.

I can't remember everything - I was dreaming promiscuously, running a lot, climbing endless ladders, necking near Rimouski.

In my more euphoric moments, with my diagnosis of + and malignant lymphoma, I feel as if I've already died and that every conscious moment is a bonus; a state of weary grace.

12

"A State of Weary Grace."

Starring.

My only regret is that everyday is not remarkable, he said.

Fuk off.

Bullshit.

I'm still writing the script of my life. It's a joke. Not a *funny* joke. A joke. A continuing *blague*. Ha, ha, ha....

I don't know what's happening....

Meanwhile, Carmen Burina and Iggy Pop are screaming through my Walkman.

My boyfriend massages my feet.

Petit M. Beauchamp, in the next bed, arrived at the General for stomach surgery but they found lung cancer. He tells somebody on the phone that he's fine. O ya, fine, just fine, perfect.

I want to stick my tongue into his mouth and shake his little body because he's a poor child of God and he's dying, lying and Honesty is the Best Policy....

Most days, he is honest, desperate, his voice thin, mangled by the oxygen. He gave a bedside performance to a group of family about God and death and described a 1971 double overtime goal by Jean Beliveau in Boston Gardens that gave me goosebumps.

I crawl under my dream between morphine gusts and lie sweating in the moonlight – ya, I'm sorry about it, this world, the bad things that hurt us. I see the white steam coming, mono-chrome buildings glisten in the dark.

Nice description. Beautiful.

It's a total lie. It's not like this at all.

It's been a long winter for many including Doris, she wants to go to Florida with Al but Al's been dead for eighteen months – she's seventy-two, eyes are blue, neuro-impaired, brain riddled with cancer, she wants to fly to Florida. Doris the butterfly. In her floral-patterned nightie.

She chants – "Pain is God. Where is Al? God is pain, Where is Al?" Every ward should have a shaman.

Down the hall a dirty-haired young man has more bags of IV than the balloon man outside the Forum. He's been here awhile; stands by my door on one leg with his Walkman before sleepy-time, silhouetted, weak and stoned, scrawled out, but *here*, joyous.

I heard him laugh once. He couldn't get his slipper on, laughing about it, hopping around and around. I laughed with him but he didn't hear me.

One weekend I shared the room with Andrew. Andrew's + too. His numbers are still fairly high although he's older, thinner than me. He has terrible pain in his gut and they can't figure it out. They removed his appendix. The surgeon patrol – a haggard group of four each with a clipboard lead by a guy who looks like a thug – visits him and asks the same questions over and over. He mumbles that he might have to go back in there, check it out....

After they go - the thug ordering yet another X-ray – Andrew comes over to my side of the room. It's Saturday night, his black cock hanging in the opening of his pajamas. He lies on my bed, his elbow on my IV under the blanket, almost rips it out of my hand. He talks about queers and clubs, things he used to do. His breath is cold and slightly adenoidal. He says he wants to die this spring, got some pills put away.

I think that he said this last year.

Not true, this is a complete fabrication.

I stare at the hockey game on tv, we've scored, yea; I pump morphine into my hand.

There are people praying for me in Kentucky.

A guy from work sent another urn of pink roses.

Andrew sighs and returns to his bed. Everyday his boyfriend brings stuffed animals to keep him company. I've been offered a caterpillar. As a symbol of rebirth, cocoons, healing/curing and all that. He moans, presses fluff into his stomach before passing out, snoring softly.

I whisper over him as he sleeps, Taoist chants I heard on PBS.

Despite myself, I recover.

The specialists snap through the curtains like comedians.

The halls whisper punch lines.

I hate the smell here.

I'm thirsty, so thirsty.

One afternoon they dig for marrow in the top of my hip. For soup. I hear a grinding noise. A group of students are laughing at my peachy butt....

I should make a will, write something about my dust, an appreciation of the mercy of family, nurse and friend but I'm fed up; I barely watch the game or listen to CJAD's Jim Duff interview a man from New York who teaches cats to shit in toilets.

The evening before I leave the hospital, Dr. Cenci, a hematologist, sits on the windowsill talking about blood. A UFO ahhs and dadas behind him in the marmalade sky. He says my white corpuscles are increasing abnormally in my blood. He says I probably have non-Hodgkin's disease, malignant lyphoma. He thinks I may have to undergo chemo although that may not be suitable considering my HIV status. He will consult.

I thank him and shake his hand before he leaves; comrade, headmaster, executioner and pal. I decide not to believe him.

I will phone the man on tv with the remarkable teeth and the cash.

In the core of the night, I wake up sweaty, possessed by lucidity and a cold sense about what Dr. Cenci has said.

I hear M. Beauchamp's seething oxygen machine. He's snorting like a colt. The herniated professor across from me has fallen adrift with the light on and his lap-top about to tumble into the sea.

Magically, one of the nurses drifts into the room, fixes up the prof, shuts off his machine. She's wearing white overalls, a scarlet wig and carries a tray with a drooling syringe for me. Is it 100 mgs? I ask. Of course, she says. I like her because she's cheerful, talks like JoJo the tv astrologer and doesn't get churchy about *Demerol*, just injects, turns off the lights, goodnight, sweet dreams.

Before dawn, I press my skull against the window at the porter's station, scare the kid they hire for the weekend.

A week later I'm in Puelo's café. I carry a smirk as I shuffle to the cash, no pain in my stomach. When people ask what's up I stutter through the clichés – a day at a time, glad to be alive, take things as they come, blah, blah, blah – I haven't seen any movies like this, that's the problem.

In the mirror, an idiot's grin. Who is that guy? I gotta put another hole in my belt. My pants don't fit. Just eat, eat anything you want, anytime – that's what the doctors said – put on the flesh, go to the *Green Spot*, demand your favourite table.

This afternoon Mathieu, my soft-hearted therapist, has to tell a young guy, twenty-five, that he's +.

He never gets pissed-off, at least near me. I'm pissed-off all the time. He said that's normal....

16

It's not normal, it's not fuking normal. Nothing about this is normal.

He's waiting for me to break down and weep.

Has anyone ever jumped from this building? That is the question.

Who cares.

I don't know what that means.

On *Fashion TV,* an expert from Paris says that serious issues are being explored by today's designers.

Some actually know what's happening, some don't, it doesn't matter; most saints don't strut and don't need cologne.

I wear *Brut.* I used to play ball-hockey.

People like me watch and wait for an empty space.

A sickening weary fatalism.

The menthol from Mathieu's cigarette is sweet and burns my throat.

Ever wonder what Mathieu's + guy is thinking tonight?

That he's a dead man, it's not right, it's not fair and will he piss all over himself and shiver in an empty room in screaming pain for centuries.

the aids guy

(For AlX)

the aids guy
doesn't want to play pool
cause the nurse cheats

she thinks
he'll feel better
if he wins

as if anything could make him
feel better:

the ripped sandwich

the blood on the lapels of strangers
as if anyone could know what it is like

the medication defrosts his lungs
and the room spins

he collapses backwards unto his berth

the ship drowns under the full moon
curses, sirens entice the wasted

passion burns only in fantasy

the young man under the *Angels* cap
leans against a pale wall of flesh

a coat of saliva and cum
over his half-hard cock

shark eyes stare into nowhere
in the blue dawn

punch drunk

18

metals & heaving hospices

broken hulls that sink
unnoticed

like pills down the white
throat into

despair

crossed
the crooked heart
hangs where memory,
a bucket of scars
and old leashes walk

masters stalk
through shingled corridors
on his back
shivering cracks that go nowhere
and never were

so we are before we were
he was, he is, he isn't

no, no name

undressed a smile

to urge a rest

to give a gun, a pill, a wrench

the wreck
the boil burst
from thirst a rabbi screams

the Christ a go-go in cheap
ceremonies
tumbles quickly into
the spirit

we are, we are, we were

& the nurse does her best

but it is the other side

where the hearts of gold
in bleeding machines
undress the wound
open the sky like smoke torn into life
inevitable dissipation
mutiny
lingering fingers

lingering tongue that no one understands
from love to this —

azt

the bitterest pill; a poison to take
to save an afternoon
lying with
the ones I love, I love, I love

the bundled hero approaches the
room with an ax and a script

he kisses the dying and turns on the tv
saying you have to watch this movie

I don't know
I'd die again to be with you

I'd kill myself to be with you

the way you smile

the love you give

Diary of A Trademark

It is an error to attempt to absent oneself from horror
because the horror swirls around anyway
even if one isn't in the high-risk group,
like nights or storms,
it dances upon the horizons
and destroys the very doors, no matter how well locked
or Victorian our sexual style.

For example - the smoke rises gracefully
from the tip of an *Export A*
at the next table
the sores of a beautiful young man
plump and suppurate
dampen the crisp coat of post-carnal
croissants in a tidy St. Denis café.
Yet in the name of Art
with the inherent beneficence of a busboy
cleaning the ashes, spilt wine and food
from the café's tables,
the conversation resumes
yet the wings are clipped
the romance wounded
the face and open laughter is now haunted.

In the nights that follow
death's face scrambles and plagues
the walls of my consciousness.
I awake screaming
almost praying that we didn't come the wrong way.
I check my nodes and shiver
certain that the zits on my arm will spread into shingles.

The snake sings

I stay away from books,
and articles in the paper about it.
Yet, yet, no matter if I read about it or not
reality obtrudes;
people dying, really dead this time
friends, acquaintances, rivals, jerks, saints, lovers.

Everybody in the bucket.

And I start to get angry
angry towards those who control the temporal;
the managers and owners of this tidy
San Fransisco-style café in the middle of Quebec swank
and the anger graduates into white screaming fury
at those who do nothing and through nothing
kill.

Ω   Ω   Ω

On the streets through a frozen December night
I remember Joe Rose,
a brave scarecrow of a boy,
high on the shoulders of another
talking about love to some confused,
uneasy tv reporter
"How's he doing" somebody asked a friend of mine
the implication, the reality behind the question,
cold and clear as the air
"He's ok", he replied.

The snake sings.

& On & On & On
On & On & On
the weird parade trudges past
indifferent cab-drivers & serious cops,
past the café & witnesses behind the glass.

We, the living, carry memory for those
who have fallen

like old soldiers without the flags,
medals or victory,
we are remembered chiefly by ourselves.

I walk with scarfed-up lesbians and
remember passing Tony & Masha
trying to light a candle.

Within 2 yrs both are dead.

& it occurs to me,
cold-boned idiot that I am,
at Tony's memorial service
that churches were created for funerals:
the sweet-voiced tenors celebrate his
friends' and family's grief.
The priest, despite his organization's
official hate policy, tries to *wrap it up*:
hypocritical bastard.

Those that love are butchered
and those who butcher are bronzed.

And the snake sings.

I get the chills

1

Paste reverse
vacuum
all horror
blood to video

subtract all terror
breath to life
dance to dance
to fuk
suk too fall

victim
on the
white stretcher

porn eclipse filled
clear morning air

stunk
smoke and mucus

slow white curtains
a young Mr. Misery

breathing the pores
I don't care about
miseries

are dying, really dead
this time

paste reverse vacuum all horror
I wait in the light
side of death.

2

Hilton sleeps
stretched and dreaming,
his soft breath pushing his heart
his red ass bruised and wet
unshaven jaw and greasy hair

and then his scent and the cigarettes evaporate.

And I'm
Here.

Now,
sort of.

And the only reminder of him are the stains
the scars
the video...

I switch it off, change the sheets, it's over.

I had the chills.

Last night, I had the chills again thinkin' about how happy I
was. I smelt like rotten meat and heard sweat screaming through
the walls.

These cheap motels, every day is a cheap motel.

I don't remember his face but I remember everything else.

It was cold, room 21. We had to be quick but it was good,
it was ok.

Hilton smirked and said "It wasn't good. It wasn't ok...."

Nobody was dancing. The lights caught his sweat under his eyes.
"I wanted to tell you before...."

He licked the splif and lit it up, sucked and held it for me.

"...I tested +."

Hilton's eyes were murky and he wasn't smiling. I took the splif, looked at it.

He started laughing but looked messed up, his eyes climbing, he broke to his knees grabbing his shoulders, pulling himself tighter and tighter.

I tell him to get up, everybody's +, big deal, big deal.

I remember Hilton laying down in the Wellington tunnel. When he was a kid. When his mother drank herself into the Douglas.

I told him about my sister's kidneys; needs a transplant. I told him about my extortionist buddies; Hodgkins, lymphoma, lesions. I look at it like night's fallen. I say something about Fuzzy-Wuzzy was a bear, Fuzzy-Wuzzy had no hair.

Chemo, chemas, chemat, chemamus. chematus, chemunt.

Sometime. Next week at the Vic. Chemo *Home Comfort.* KeyMo.

I don't think Bobby cares how I look at it. Or my pathology at this moment. He's +. That's what matters.

I slap him across the face a couple of times, his hair whipped back.

3

I push my foot to the floor, the *Cougar* gently climbs over the meridian, off the Ville Marie through the night sky towards the milky way, flipping into a triple somersault, bursting into fiery clouds of disintegration high above the earth.

Or run over by an 18-wheeler in Lennoxville, at the bend near the bridge over the Massawippi near the college.

I'd like to swallow a pill, overdose on heroin in Parc LaFontaine like Henn, that spring night; misadventure along with *Le Boulevard des Reves Cracke*.

Put a barrel between my lips, shoot the back of my skull against cheap wallpaper at the Siesta Motel in Niagra Falls.

But I don't because I remember David. And what I heard he did to squeeze out each day.

I never met him.

But he had some reason.

I'm a disciple.

4

Hilton got up before I could hit him again and took me outside. We slipped and fell in the street.

We had coffee near the Forum and talked about vitamins. He's taking freeze-dried premium blue-green algae capsules. He said he'll be alright, his blue eyes crossed and wet. He was broke again.

The lady at the cash says I made five dollars and seventy-five cents picking *loto* numbers. I forgot I was part of a syndicate with twelve strangers who signed this form at MultiMag. They came looking for me with a crisp five dollar bill and three quarters in an orange envelope.

She said I was a lucky man.

It's true, I'm *trés* lucky!

I barked at Hilton and ordered another round of bacon. *Pour Toutes Mondes!*

(Hilton makes me bark, I feel like pissing over fire-hydrants when I see him. I was so yap-yap Yappy Happy! – Maybe we could work out a suicide-pact!)

I love winning *loto*-money, it's so fuking cool. Freeee Money!

I would have loved someone to come into the greasy café at this point to share the bacon bonus, my porcine largesse, with Hilton and this merry crowd of artistes and poets; a wrestler perhaps, a drunk rookie from the Expos, a secret agent, a couple of floosies, the aids guy, Monique, Francis Bacon, John Huston, but I have to sleep now.

Maybe I could have a struggle, a café brawl before I sleep.

A big brawl with the cashier pouring red-hot black coffee over the wrestler's fat face. And Hilton tossing Ralph Gustafson through the glass.

But no one entered and Hilton kept getting more and more morose until he couldn't stop laughing.

I left a huge tip, took a worn packet of matches from the counter and a wallet.

"Hey, it's mine", a voice gets choked by the closing door.

Of course, it is.

Hilton says he dreams about a beluga trapped in a draining fjord and the receding tide, smiling and blowing steam, admired by naturalists, photographed by tourists, blissfully doomed.

He sleeps on my sofa and cries over the weekend. I offer him *Serax,* a tranquilizer, a valium-type pill but he doesn't sleep. He eats. Cries and eats. I look at his plate – the niblets floating in white spume.

His earhole's wider; I can put a finger through it now. It's infected.

5

The room downstairs has green flies crawling over the computers.

They are warm with purpose; flies are attracted to this and suck energy through their antennae as they waddle across the grey screens.

I am working on a cure for aids in the downstairs room.

I'm analyzing international medical data around the clock. I collect acronyms.

I keep falling asleep but I can't sleep.

I don't want to do Key-Mo.

My hair falls out. One by one, the green flies carry them off and build a soft nest in the tower over the market near the meat vendors and the acupuncture school.

6

I advise Hilton to see a therapist. Stress must be reduced. Absolutely. And stop eating crap. Like bacon and fuking eggs.

We discussed buying some coke but I hate coke so we bought half a splif out of my loto winnings and got stoned at my place, fell asleep for a couple of hours. Later, walked along the canal. Saw a rich guy's pug eating a pigeon in the snow.

When I got back I woke Hilton and we drove through the Wellington tunnel, ended up on the mountain looking for the mansion where our friend fell off the roof.

dear Sir

dear Sir I got off the bus and purchased a bus-ticket to Santa Monica.

Just like you said.

The boy was bleeding from his nose down his chin and into the sea.

I dumped my gear on yr verandah and walked twenty-one blocks to Ocean Blvd and then another ten blocks south to Venice.

Just like you said.

Pulled the belt open and dropped the heroin on the sand.

I went for a swim after two and a half days on the buses. The sand was very hot and I couldn't see properly because it was so bright. Trying to act cool while blind and feet burning and then I fell and almost drowned. Didn't know what I was doing, caught up in the current and the whole Californian thing, actually being here and some big wave knocked me over onto my shoulder and I couldn't get up.

Just like you said.

The gayboys on the beach won't spend anything on me. I am ugly compared to them. And my shoulder's sore so I grimace. I bought five pairs of sunglasses because they were cheap. Three dollars. American.

Was that alright?

The guy on the skate board took the heroin.

The ambulance took the boy's body on a rubber tray. The food on this beach is greasy. I need to get in shape. I always say that but I *have* to now. Tomorrow may be too late.

You say that. Sometimes. When they've finished your dialysis. *Tomorrow may be too late.* And I lift you up the screaming stairs, past the swaying dim blue bulb. In the warehouse of the skins, you mumble quietly; exhausted by the treatment, your stomach is sore from the plugs. I undress you and lay you on the cot and clean sheets. I throw a blanket over you, dear sir.

Sleep, perchance to dream

dear Sir

I wait outside the door listening to *Nine Inch Nails* through my earphones. Sometimes I check my gun or leaf through Harrowsmith.

You have wide interests. I will protect you from disturbance while you rest, regaining your strength.

Just like you said.

Ω   Ω   Ω

I'm on the beach. In Venice. Smoking *DuMaurier.*

Ready.

It is perfect to stay here. In America.

The skin on your back is peeling and must be replaced by cool hands gloved in *Armani* deer skin.

My skin is pink and hot, to be honest – felt like I was living in a pond up north, in Quebec; the humidity and the cold made me cough and the snow wasn't so bad, it was the stunk air clawing my lungs, the brown slush around the ankles, the car lights diffused in the gas.

In the gas I see dogs playing on the edge. They're not supposed to be there.

The gulls are huge and hungry and dive on each other, twisting like blenders trying to catch the grease from the sand.

The drunk, fat man yells at the birds, his bathing suit stretched over a large belly. He looks like my father; his red face, his lazy lips.

Do you want to go in?

I've taken a video of the beach and the boys. I'll rub yr skin until you're ready and cover your face until the video-screen turns off....

Let's be dead

I know the club where you got the blow-job
I know the bleak mountain of skin
whathisname
he's been after you for years
I can hear you coming; the rolling white
the drum machine
I've tasted sour hope
in every angle
every flex
all night
it's alright
it's ok it's only a fuking blowjob

I sympathize with
the ones who won't give up

we gave up yesterday

we gave up tomorrow

I hear wings
and cathedral dogs

I know that guitars are more merciful than fate
especially the ones around yr bed

red paint trundles through yr veins now

yellow varnish shoots
over the hips of dark clouds
bitter graffiti howls in ecstasy
on a wall near McGill

poets closing in
golden careers
wait for you but not here

some idyllic meadow

some pristine moment

come to the stage
come
read us yr poems about yr travels
the experience with the slaves
who don't respect you because
you've never done anything except be rich

the slaves who flatter
the slaves who you serve

claw and foot

this is honesty and I know you can take it
yr young and tattooed and will be cut up and killed
I will kill you with my disease as you have killed me
and we will be the happier for this
dead
forever dead
if you can take a chance

if you can take a chance
you'd abandon beauty
you'd deface beauty

and become obvious and transparent

like whathisname with the good tongue and the wine
bottle playing along the lips of his damp hole as he sucks you
and you were happy because the door was locked
and he had the key
and you were thrilled because he believed you
every word about everything
when you came he said merci he thought you were French
the way you stumble and stutter over the names of the saints
in the cubicle above the glory holes

St. John the Baptist

St. Francis d'Assisi

waiting for no one special

as you washed his hands and pulled his fingers through yr hair

leaving crusts on yr sideburns

ummm, you said and I believed it, ya I believed it, all of it, even
the cock under the railway bridge, even the guys from Vancouver
who fuked you together one afternoon in a highrise

they keep calling me

you left something

a photo of you and the family at the deathbed

the caterers spilling gas on your legs

the spreading silence and someone asking you to smile for the
coroner and ummm, I believed you when you said you were a
mercenary and yr lover got his brain blown out while you were
on patrol

that's what they do now

squirming about the sexual content
while the bodies are piled to the sun

they don't understand —

you and I still believe in god and beauty and the victory of love
and the supremacy of flesh over money and ecstasy over jobs

because we are dead

infused with life they are jealous
they have rosettes attached to everything

ahhh, they have *everything*

let's go for a drive

let's be dead

c'mon

I don't care about anything now as long as we're together

grave by grave

hand to hand

we shall lay laughter on all those jerks

those fuks from seriouspoemland who want to get published

who gives a shit

and don't tell me this isn't a poem cause it is – it's just a poem
with a purpose you don't recognize cause you're overeducated I'll

kill you
if you're lucky

Wounds: Valentine's Day

Some guy put a lit cigarette into my shoulder in your storeroom. That was in October, my first time in Montreal.

When I was released into the back of the city I had five separate burns in an arc on my shoulder, so when I got back to McGill I thought about you for months, even in Rochester, my home town; it was always sore; I never really healed, always somebody scraping them open, making me bleed.

And Winnipeg, the sadistic Indian with whom I thought I was in love, soft-skinned, soft-spoken, he too made me bleed, chewing my shoulder as he shot.

But when I left him I came back to you. St. Valentine's Day, empty-hearted at last, on a perfect day, perfect for you, with the wind blowing ash off the hood of your *Buick*, with another boy auditioning on stage in your empty club.

I used to think that your eyes were blue.

I used to worry about love, where it hid when the fires tore off the door, when the rubber hands squeezed the pale thin throat.

I watched him jerk and look sexy to the disco beat and the mirrors but he took off his g-string with shaking hands, his half-hard unskinned cock escaping into light, squeezed at the base by a red suede strap. I knew that within a week you'd beat him and make him do anything for you just like you had done to me.

You lowered the music. Putting the cigarette in your mouth, you stepped over the braid unto the stage. You held the boy's elbow, instructing him, pouting at him, telling him to pose a little longer, take it easy, the customers liked that. This went on for a few minutes until you laughed charmingly.

Without being seen I ducked into the toilet.

Waiting for you to come back was like waiting for the drug to kick in, knowing I'd be somewhere else, would be someone else and I could watch it all.

Finally, you showed up. I was waiting in a cubicle and I saw you pull out your cock and spray the back of the urinal. You saw me and grunted, almost laughing. I followed you into the alley, I took off my boots, jeans and shirt and threw them into the back of your car and waited.

Like I had the first time.

After putting on your gloves you told me to get in.

I don't know this city and I don't want to. We drove through a tunnel and soon we were through the suburbs and into an industrial park on the edge of the country.

Near a river, under a bridge you taped my ankles together and my wrists behind my back, you wound tape over my eyes so I couldn't see you.

You pushed me down. The ground was wet, cold but clean.

The only thing you said was, "The Lord is my Shepherd I do not want...."

I didn't care. Even then I knew he was going to kill me; I could smell the knife as clearly as I could smell his ass. He put his cock in my mouth and knew he was going to slit my throat as he came because that is what I wanted him to do.

Roughly he shoved and lifted my legs so that he was over me with his smile poised and ready over my hole; he licked it, hit it, pulled his fist back and slugged it, then bit into my skin. I was numb when he threw his cock into my ass. He had no trouble ripping my hole and pushing it in all the way. He fuked me for a minute then took it out, put on a condom and started again.

I could feel warm liquid dribbling through my crotch. I heard ice floes on the river cracking under each other. Gradually, I forgot what was happening. The tape started to come off my eyes and I could see lights, some buildings in the dark distance.

After he came he emptied the condom on my head and kissed me, his thin lips wired with nicotine, sharp nicotine, tongue so warm.... I could feel his juice sliding down the neck over my throat.

He took out the knife. He cut the tape off my ankles and hands.

But I don't care about freedom. Not when I'm with him.

Without a word, I knew he knew but it wasn't going to be easy. He shoved me towards the car. "You can work in the basement tonight."

He wouldn't let me touch my dick even though it was dark red and harder than cement. He gave me a blanket and told me to be quiet.

I started shaking as the street lights slid over my shoulders. I could feel the salt burning where you had scraped me. I knew that my arc was now bleeding and probably wouldn't heal. Ever.

You put on a tape; *ChemLab* – the music tore through my ears as we tore through the tunnel. I mouthed the words as Jared, the singer, shouted "I Still Bleed, I Still Bleed" over and over. I knew that song, it was our song, darling, *our* song.

I looked down and pulled the blanket away from my groin. I slid forward and my cock throbbed like a fat fish on a plate. I knew that you'd like to cut it off and eat it. I knew that you were going to shave my crotch and make me lie in the shower in the basement on a leash and drink a hundred men. As a special treat for all the members. And at dawn you'd let me be fuked by twelve men, friends or rich ugly bastards and when it was over, when even the young boy who auditioned this afternoon had shot his thick load over my back and screamed, slamming his balls over my wide open hole, that you'd burn me, perhaps in the same place, perhaps on my face, perhaps when I was unconscious, perhaps when I was open-eyed and hungry.

I looked over your face as we emerged from the underground. Except for the scar, it was unlined and content. At that moment you could have been my younger brother Jeff, the one working at *Kodak* as a mechanical designer, the shutter specialist.

I wonder what Jeff would think of his brother, the burn-freak, the queer. Or if he'd care. I can't remember ever thinking about what he does with his dick.

I'd rather hear slashing guitars and feel a cool orange butt on my flesh, the incense of flesh, flesh and smoke....

I don't want to ever shoot. I want to be hard for you always, naked, taped tight and burnt for you.

I still bleed, I still bleed

Such is my love, my love, my love....

So my cock burned. At a traffic light you looked at it and slapped it hard, hurting me. When it wouldn't go down, you squeezed my balls and it hurt too much, I almost passed out.

Almost. Almost.

On the edge.

Of *Never.*

I thought I was going to die until I didn't think at all. My brain was full of pain and there was nothing else.

As it was when you burnt me, on my shoulder, on an arc, five stars.

Sell that guitar
you'll never learn to play
yr hole
you gave to some punk
    with an XL cock

He called a meeting to watch you bleed

the last time I saw you was on *MuchMusic*
in my jacket
yr skin covered in a rash of innocence

2 wks later
broke, thin, the record deal - forget it
the money, the big deal
whatta joke

2 wks later
back in my fuking bed

everything is cracking you said
and the punk is on my phone for you
you are naked except my leather jacket
and a hard-on

the Holy Son of Nowheretown
returns to the scene of the fatal accident

I pull on yr balls with my lips
you force my mouth back to the cock
and start

across the city

I feel better
thanks for letting me fuk you

Come now
shoot over my hair
shoot
and we will be free
you can have the punks
I'll take my jacket
go to the club
and forget yr music

forget yr dirty ass
forget yr acned skin

the pictures you paint with razors

Let us devour ourselves
on the table near the river
on plastic plates and checkered tablecloths;
our reflections on the dome of the sugar-dispenser
our fatal accident
our love
our secret
broadcast on the tables of unanswered telephones;
anything is better than that motel

come crash with me, come crash

even you, scarfaced and stupid

I don't care if he's thin; I take care of him when he's cold
I watch the stupid shows on tv just to share time with him

I'm tired of what the waitresses and every dime-store pope
has to say about Timmy, about Jimmy, dimmy, creamy, crack

I can't stand it
but I'm not alone anymore

I wear spurs and get drunk, now I belong, now I am someone
in this small town
I got friends across the hall, they like us
They don't care if we're only an accident.

We dine at the *New System Restaurant*
Good people pay extra for quality and *New System* delivers
I order some onion rings because I know they're awful
and probably crawling with carcinogens

There are lines on my lover's eyes, wounds of time, I guess
wounds of time – What the hell does that mean?
He's watching sports on tv, I hate sports;
can't abide their victories, let's get outta here—

where's the fuking waitress?

Forget Love

bodies in the hallway
fluorescent inmates on the edge
stretched and back

fuking like gutting
fish the flesh
chuffed

uh, it's great

7 tonight, # 7

looks like Sebastian

fuks like a machine

forget love
leave the skin behind
I don't need it
when I'm fuking
Sebastian

After the cum in the cubicle
with the vinyl bed
with ash on my ass
cum drooling down my chin....

Ω   Ω   Ω

Out of the baths
into the street
a Cougar coasts
past Lévesque & Wolfe
in the bucket seat
a hustler
takes it deep
like a pony in the manger

Creeping walls

Wet cockroaches
shuffle up and down the screen
the porno flick stutters

gristled cocks
blink
as the camera
pours over their bodies

shooting over some guy's
guy over and over
bodies and bodies
skin, skin, skin.

The soldier is inspired
beats off in the dark
in a stall, his slim body convulsed
over the door like
a tortured pup

Ω   Ω   Ω

brief lives,
the man shoots up my nostrils,
wipes my lipstick off with his cock
the brains melting meat
black and gold
crumble
tumble

*"At that instant I understood that a calamity had hit us, that we were
beginning a period of rampant misfortune from which there would be no
escape."* *

*– Herve Guibault, To a friend who didn't
save my life, *High Risk Press*

**Doctors, don't tell it to him that way -
say it but don't put it like that.**

I prepare my body
I prepare my skin
I wrap myself in milk and egg
cover myself in bread crumbs
delicate spices and herbs

fresh rabbit
on a steel bed

dripping barium out my ass
tipping one way and the next
the mechanical fist pounding me
into clay
warm with cancer

growing under my jaw

What's yr count
how are you *feeling* how are you *feeling*

I *feel* like Milan/New York/Paris/Toronto is setting the scene with
fashion
I *feel* it's where I want to be right now; he makes me feel sexy like
a woman sexy

Mona

I *feel* many people care but can't
do a fuking thing
about this disease

I *feel* there's a level of irony about this
I'm too stupid to catch

I *feel* useless

I *feel* like a jerk although pleased to serve the community in any
way possible.

O my people

Dreams of Clots

Napalm dances over the cow,
leaping from it's surprised haunches,
trying to shake it off like a fly.

Everybody's afraid to die.
Life valued above all else.

They should use *Chanel* on the body bags;
death could be glamorous again —
varnished fingers and glitzy memorial services, flags,
bags and Maria Callas screaming, cursing at the cameras on the
runways in *Tosca* drag

twirling blood drunk through the killing fields
as we have for centuries

genocide, rape, murder, cowardice

Ratty is hiding under his desk, Ratty is burying somebody or
killing somebody, a big weapon bolted under his arm, Ratty is a
fascist, nationalist, big boots and knife, dreams of clots, his
massacred village, his dear mother raped by Muslims/Serbs/
Croats, his son boned and salted for snacks along the Rhine

Lord Owen is talking
he says it is very complicated and he is a sincere man

The dead boy is talking
he says it is very complicated but that the people must never
surrender!

Never Surrender!

The dead don't go out enough, don't understand what's
happening

They become condiments served in thimbles

At the baptism the infant's throat opened, torso drained.

The New Europeans gather by the Fountain of Martyrs
drinking, listening to the General recite Shelley.

A tear in his eye; he doesn't remember why he was born.
It's easy to forget

mortar fire sinking through the hospital
children, nurses, doctors showered with blood and tissue.

Horror everywhere
overflowing the world

shattered

In the meadows the soldiers are burning cows.
They cannot be controlled.

The poet withdraws to the shack and watches animals melt
at sunset.

Ratty is a survivor,
even if there is war,
it will be his neighbour's daughter with a broken heart
riddled with steel.

Not him.

Tonight he will give the order to burn the village.

It is unfortunate but
it is a very complicated situation and from the outside may
seem quite absurd but in a historical context, when understood
as part of an ongoing political evolution....

The herded wolves, bold only to pursue;
The obscene ravens, clamorous o'er the dead. *

                                        *Shelley, **Adonais**

Song of the Legs of Nicaragua

I am a boy, thirteen years old. My name is Oscar de la Chaigua. Last year I rode my bike through San Diego and everybody was staring at me because it was the first time anyone had ever rode a bike without legs. Someone stole my legs while I was sleeping in a big ranch-style property belonging to Mr. and Mrs. Shoulderstoy. I was visiting this delightful couple on my scholarship to a private Mission school.

Anyway, I rode all over town; into the center with the park along the beautiful river and then to the world-famous zoo where they filmed the begining and end of "Three's Company " with John Ritter and Susanne Sommers and, of course, Don Knotts who is the funniest guy alive. I had a fantastic time and I'd like to thank the Shoulderstoys, their lovely daughter, Krista and handsome son, Derek, for being so hospitable to me, a little boy from the mountains in North Nicaragua.

What is misfortune? Can anyone truly say that I have suffered misfortune. Yes, I have lost my legs and it is true that I cannot help my family in the fields. It is true that we are very poor and live in a shack not far from where they spray. But I can tell you this - I take up less room now. They have cut my bed in half and Teresa, my youngest sister does not need to sleep on the floor anymore. To help your sister, your family, that is not misfortune. I help my aunt with the food. We are honest people. (The Shoulderstoys are very honest, too; Mr. Shoulderstoy works very hard to support his family. He is away from his family and that must be terrible considering how much time our family is together. He is a skinsurgeon, a Doctor who can make actors and stars very young and beautiful. It is very hard work and very important and he is an honest man. Mrs. Shoulderstoy has terrible trouble with her skin; Mr. Shoulderstoy cut her face open and successive skin transplantations only made it worse so the burdens hang very heavily over this fine family. Derek has mental problems and must take lots of cocaine to help him stay awake during the night when he is working on music. He makes beautiful music which scares me because it sounds like bombs and stomachs being ripped by the sharp machetes of Somoza's soldiers. I tell him this and he laughs. I like Derek very much. He will be a great musician.)

I feel my legs sometimes when I am dreaming. I am running and can feel their muscles and I am running fast and my ankles gliding in the air and touching and bouncing again through the air. I am a cat. Sometimes I dream I am a cat.

I am stupid. Teresa says sometimes I am whining in my sleep. In my little cot.

In San Diego I had my own room. I slept on silk but I could not dream on their beds. I had a room and they hacked off my legs. The Shoulderstoys gather around my bed and even the Sandanistas spit at me and they do not buy my father's cane anymore because they say that I am an American now.

They macheted my legs by the pool at a large party for Mr. Shoulderstoy's wedding anniversary. A big party and they had a Mexican band and everybody drank tequila and even Derek was laughing. He offered me some coke but it isn't a good drug, something wrong with American coke, it's poisoned I think, by the people who sell it. Anyway I helped set up the tables, raked the back, cleaned the pool. They always smile when I help them and once Mrs. Shoulderstoy gave me money and I sent it home but the government took it from my father, said since the Americans were robbing the country, they owed the people at least something in return. I want to know why my family suffers, why the sides of the trees are black with blisters and tears.

I went to the Rose Bowl last year. Shirley Temple Black was the Queen of the parade. I remember the old movies sometimes they showed in the church basement. I thought all American girls were like Shirley Temple. She is a good dancer and she'd make everybody laugh and forget about our problems for awhile.

My mother laughed, too. I waved at Shirley Temple and she kissed me lightly on the forehead.

She tucked the hood over my head.

50

I love her.

When I came to San Diego I thought I would visit her but the Shoulderstoy's just laughed when I said I wanted to see her. They said you can't just walk up to Shirley Temple Black; she's a big star, besides, she's in L.A.

Don't be shocked by the idea of a party in the backyard of a rich San Diego suburb with tequila, live Mexican music, tacos and dip where they hold you down and hack off the legs of a thirteen year old boy from the mountains of Nicaragua. It did not hurt at all because they drugged my legs so they fell asleep and did not hurt when Dr. Shoulderstoy swung the sharp machete and hacked off my left leg. Derek was bothering his father to do the right leg but Dr. Shoulderstoy only let him have a swing after three attempts had not broken the bone. The blood was shooting out all over the place but the maid had covered the picnic table with a plastic covering and some of the neighbourhood kids were grimacing and hosing away all the loose skin, bone fragments and dark, rich blood. There was a great cheer and congratulations when Derek pulled off the right leg. Everybody was cheering and laughing and Derek's aunt took photographs of the guests and the Sholderstoys. I was in the centre. I wasn't feeling the best; I looked a bit white but some young doctors stitched up my open wounds, carving neat points and spraying anti-bacteria stuff all over. The smiles on their faces showed that they cared about my well-being and that I shouldn't worry and that I was the star of San Diego at that particular moment. They pointed to the video camera and encouraged me to wave and smile. I don't want to be a star, I said, but they just laughed and the nurses wrapped up my stumps at mid-thigh, they even put a beautiful purple ribbon around them.

I looked at my little legs on the concrete veranda. My feet had on high-tops. From *Converse*. I think Michael Jordan wears *Converse*. I don't know.

After a couple of more minutes taking pictures and video, Dr. Shoulderstoy gave a signal and one of the big, tall men in sunglasses and wearing Hawiian shirts, came and took me upstairs. He wasn't gentle or drunk. He threw me on my bed. A nurse gave me shots and the next thing I knew I was back in my family's home and Tomisita, our terrible cat, was licking my damp stumps.

Joe

His blood
livid as lava
his heart stuck in thorn
cradles knives slash
innocent stones
burst smoke
sunk into the murk
of murder

While the country slurps the slurring condiment, sour-cream
crab diplomacy, the cocktail repression, the bridle of style and
reserve stuck through a glory hole, the pundits and professional
mediocrity compromise into cronies in blue Bay suits selling
the country like heroin with humour and resignation they get
on the fx and beat the drums, keeping themselves occupied
with small triumphs, little dramas, profits;

Mulroney's cheap lives & his cheap visions

shoving the chair shoving the chair shoving the CHAIR I don't care

just nod my head against the wall, nod my head against the wall;
the junkie barely asked slumps to the blood-stained linoleum
floor, his point well-taken

Get up, rise, you stunk asses creep junkie slime-veined pathetic
excuse for baby's meadow and a picnic under the trees

Abandon Nelson Eddie and the foaming minstrel choir

My hair creeps when I think of you

My country is a drug clinic haunted by despair and the abused
strung along the border, spiritless, a run-over snake;
luminescent and torn,

the nurses whisper, drop a word; the clots move to the bowels.

The knives *score.*

Maniacal screams tear through the frigid wilderness.

My country, intent on murder/suicide.
As the bus slides through the streets the boys take out their
knives, wheels spinning crazily, the uniforms of chaos stream
and hush over their smiling, excited faces

Names end
through the city
the song machine glows.

The blizzard heals the glorious finale, the cum-stretched
Bonnie & Clyde resolution, the cinema of romance.

Sleepless nights bent over the driving wheel explode into
laughter and blood; the drunkless fire and limbs caught in the
flashing light;

My country intent on war

swaddled in white

Ω   Ω   Ω

The boy gets up on stage at the Idiot Bar and starts singing
about fuking somebody.

Nobody told him that Northrop Frye died.

Goodbye Mr. Frye. In the time of sausages well-bred or
wrought, glossing to the jig, the hornbill glows, tapped, stapled,
stung braids in Mayday twists, clamoring to someone about
anatomy;

and the voices we heard

the St. Francis river dead
to the core, the very veins poisoned

The glamour of wisdom, goodbye Mr. Frye —
It is a bad sign when the wisest retire
when the owls sweep away at dawn
leaving only the vague glow of fangs
in the night sky
over an endless bed of tundra
and Gordon Lightfoot songs.

Out of control: the weird images of
millionaires singing "give peace a chance"
the huge fatty florid head and thin lips
of Joe Clark, the warrior dunce.
B/W grainy images of exploding buildings
Military camouflage enjoying celebrity status
Canadian fighter jets providing escort
to American bombers over Iraq

thus we are innocent of righteousness

tongues ripped from our mouths.

They have dismantled the country slice by slice
the tracks
the airlines,
history rewound and flushed

Ω   Ω   Ω

on the bus

beaten, infected, kicked to death

by boys from all over the world

from Verdun

on a bus

with frenzied knives

back and forth

they cut him to pieces

from Verdun

Good Friday

Good Friday

cut him to pieces

Butchered

one after the other taking slices

Joe

draining from the wounds

the cops with his body still in the aisle
asking the boys a few questions

Dream #2

In the end we traveled on our own

through faithless memories
into the garden

posing by the pool of coloured syrup
with the men I knew from the health club

the waiters served meat

I don't think you understand

I throw my skin away like a wet towel

it's worthless

you don't understand

I want to assassinate a bad guy

instead of myself

shoot someone special

instead of myself

in the name of God

instead of myself

I started to get sick in New York...

(for David Wojnarowicz)

Ah, I started to get sick in New York
started to cough all the time.
Everytime I looked out the window
cold cold rain.
I knew it was time to get back
so I packed up and gave a cold dry kiss to this guy,
knew I'd never see him again.
And I carry across the city
and I carry across the state
and I remember
the sweet nights,
the books of my mistakes

and what about the dreams
what about the dreams?

A cold light rain
slides against the pane
and suddenly the world is full of numbers
as I watch my numbers fall.
And I hear knots and I hear screaming,
I hear the dogs all the time
and there's a young man opposite me
and he looks like you
hollow eyes that know,
yes we know
how the soldiers will fall.

And I just wanted to write to tell you
that I'm doing ok I guess.
People have been very kind.
I have dreams,
still dream
but try to let em fall
and I never find my ticket.
Have you seen my ticket?

Barely know who I am
if you could send me a photo
I'd appreciate it
cause there are tigers around my bed
and I feel needles in my head
and I'm waving goodbye
it's like my skin is on fire....
Someone is dancing down the hall
and I hear music
death dance all
and I'm just waving goodbye
just waving goodbye....

Brief Doorways

(for Francis Bacon)

went into La Folie, sorely sauced
ordered two more, cursed Jean and looked

around the plump lady in barbed tongue
offers me an opportunity to buy her a beer
but I tastefully decline: old drag.

Did not roll in this bar, did not
skunk, did not trundle or stumble.

I am innocent.

These good-willed narcs, pounding
my back, harkness,

nurd-ball drug-snifters, old stiff-wind,
stainless fukheads.

I sang a song with Jim but he
couldn't play and Mark couldn't play.

I hung like a kite
pushed one verse
through
it all.   I am sick.   I am being watched.

We stop playing.
The waiter tells me to be careful,
so do they all:
careful, careful
as I carefully fall apart.

Confused chrome boxes
trundle aimlessly down the hospital lanes.

I go bowling there often
with Mr. Won't
professor from the Institute

I'd rather be a drunk than a Zombie.

I'm sick, I hear
knots

I walk home, clanking motorcycle jacket.

What an idiot.

Through the November winter
along St. Antoine

I don't see anybody

just some model
staring at me from a huge billboard.
I know him but I don't understand
what he's doing there.

Sometimes it makes sense
sometimes
I sorta get a handle...
most of the time it's all just
fuked.

My left eye is starting to shake
uncontrollably, it trembles.

My head is like the globe —
they're poisoning me, it's true—
earthquakes and toxic dumps and nuclear
waste and butchered skies—
I can see why my friend just does
drugs and watches tv.

I can see why I'm dead.

My ears are frozen as cockroaches
take urine samples from around the bowl

The cats scream
still
locked
I am a stick
in a basement
bathed in tv waves.

I pull out my cock
I tie a boot-lace around my balls

  A dog leads a forest-fire rescue.
  A bad man is shot.
  Mia falls for Mel.
  Let Jes-Uz into Yr life.

I shoot and fall asleep

Study for self-portrait # 2

Ecstasy rode the metro looking for love; every door slid open possibilities, crotches and cute faces, jeans and white slacks, leather jackets, sweat pants and earrings. He imagines what their cocks look like, what they would do when they came, the shape of their faces as they shot inside him, the pubic hatch and the tongue caressing the balls of the zit-faced hunk coming home from hockey, pulling the skin over the fat, blunt head of his dick.

He would often get hard and he would have to sit down, so hard every decent citizen could lick it with their eyes if they saw.

Ecstasy walked around his room in red boots and a whistle in his mouth. The white furry pussy with the green eyes stared into the middle distance and smoked a long cigarette. The white-tie butterflies moved from the columns and began to tremble with the fire and the music in the centre of the universe. All the shops closed early. All the trains ran in one direction, the flagship of all grade B science fiction Emperors hovered as Ecstasy fondled his cock with his legs hanging over the side of a sky-scraper and looked at the people below, the huge mass of humanity. Above him helicopters and pleasure craft, cruisers and bruisers and airline stewards, looking on, watching. Ecstasy pulled it out of his pants. He was always semi-hard and dripping. He wasn't the type to get shriveled up over nothing - most men, it seemed to him, had to come from a state of fear to his state of ecstasy, had to pull extra to reach his normal state of heat.

They didn't cum any different than him but needed more time, more manipulation. Ecstasy ran a fingertip between the slit on the thick-hooded head of his penis, pulling a clear drop of precum to the tip of his tongue. He could drown in the very taste of it. Ah, could there be anything more joyous? All the warriors, all the governments of mere flaccid power-brokers and torturers, autocrats, religious princes and fashion stars, Hollywood stars, glittering artists - they should get back to the juice. He thought that if everybody would just consider their juices as more important than anything else, everything would be just splendid, practically perfect.

Gods & junkies

pockets full of glue
into the clinic

they know you

needing your help
down the long arm
to the laughing door
and their cots
row upon row

where will they go?
where have they been?
where is here and here is nowhere

Have a shower in the metal cage
shave the days and scrub the river

the thin gristled ribs
of the good life

There are movies men die for
There are moments I have to see

not just your balls in a leather box,
not just your lips on cassette.

Rewind the tape and you'll see. You are a human being.
You, you move your lips. Now you are drinking a *Coca-Cola.*
You look great. Look at that jaw, whew.... Those lips. Oh man.
You are a god of lips.

There are movies people die for
There are moments I have to see

Life is too cold, Monique, Monique

So we drove back
carried on the long lights,
the long highway lights

to the inborn
nation of the unbred
city of the indead home, to home,
through the tunnel of unfinished phrases
up the screaming stairs to the dim blue bulb
swaying in the warehouse of the skins

I tie my wrists with knotted leather
My hands are tied

Please Stand for the Playing of the National Anthem

I stand for Nothing
New Images? No. New Music? No. New Hands? No

I squat in courage

In the back where nobody goes, nobody talks, a cold wind blows

I await the
slow steps of the
indead
voice

scratches every horizon, it says -
I don't believe....
I don't believe in it anymore.

I have eaten from the wise eyes
the glistening eyes; spooned the greedy eyes,
marbled baby's eyes of the hero's waiter
in a wrinkled land
to home, to home

So we returned after discovering
America is an ugly town.
I stare in the star-spangled eyes and
see a parking-lot,
long fin cars, rusty shopping carts and weeds
busting through the concrete.

John Huston is Dead
that's all I know.

This is the face no one wants
this is the face that you forgot.
In yr eyes
I see myself
a cigarette, a shattered bottle on the sidewalk,
the flame strapped to the warehouse of yr skin
hung by the throat of yr cold, hard breath

home, to home

Life is too cold Monique, Monique
and I don't believe in it

I wait for it but don't believe in it.

Preparing

When the fire got to my throat
I swallowed

the flesh does what it wants
the veins broiled
lungs baked
brain spoilt
while the heart hunts for dogs
scratches into love

the flesh does what it wants
and forever

the asylum reeks of disease

the young sceptic
stares and waits for chemo
with all the others
his levels falling
his kidneys hurt slowly at odd hours.

Where are the words that could save
each tear, a year
throbbing with anger.

Would I rather be discovered
frozen pale and stiff in the woods

or stumbling blind through agony
tubes and deathbed extravaganzas;

the hell of hospices?

At this time I leave the door open
the cold untouched

I have lost control.

This bus is accelerating faster than planned

Come crash come crash come crash with me.

I heard HIV
and lymphoma cancer
have been seen together dancing
surreptitiously
by the river

which is great cause I live there
a minute from the beach

it was beautiful there
once
it was —

St. Henri   05/04/94

Say it, say it

I could drown in the beauty of his lips

drown not far, not far

from here
where the cars tumble
where the clips, tv colours
die

sweet reason sweet reason
the oil that preserves
the gloved hand that strangles my cock between
falling walls;
a truly comprehensive treatment
between low arches and funhouse boys

I could drown here under his tongue between ecstasy and his
laughter between his shivering crack and the departure under his
memory and the funeral and somebody else who suks me badly
and whose fat dirty meat carries ungainly desperation like a nerd
looking for a musical chair, desperately pink with his grip pulling
it, pulling it horribly until the cream is finally squeezed out, the
poor thin boy closes his eyes in exhaustion and I want to kill him
as his meat shrinks back into the teenage bush and I continue to
fuk his face until he *can't* until he surrenders, bends over and
takes it and I only fuk him because he doesn't care, doesn't know
that I won't ever release him, not until he is hard again, screaming
for justice, screaming for nothing but my cock, shoved as deep as
a rifle up his neverland ass....

And when he screams for nothing else I will tear it through him
and depart, pulling it out like a bayonet and he will suffer through
my absence even as I ride another and they shall all scream while I
fuk the line between twilight and glory

all the boys go fish

68

<u>the way the want ads look at you</u>
it's a good life if you're dead

        getting a feel for it
                   like everyone else looking
             like I was crazy dogs wandering sideways
    exhausted
               along St. Denis my pyro friend giggles,
               squats on his haunches pissing through
               his pants and trying to light up a
               garbage bin

     l o s   t

              getting back to the mutt, ok
      he was like lost.

 Somebody's fuking godog man
  sorta half mad kept like stepping over the curb between the
  parked cars but the oncoming lights freaked it out you know
back and he was dead dog man....That's the *pathetic,* that's the
most *pathetic* uh thing, *pathetic, pathetic,*

Anyway he started looking back at me like a want ad and I
gained valuable working experience with commission

I did the mirrors, bannisters, tables, toilets, the sink,

cup, my cup, took a sip from it, looked at my eyes in the light,

watched the prince in his bloody apron shave his head,

listened to the striptease in the catscan,

I've dined here

and died here

feeling it out as I go along
like everybody else

winning lottery numbers

we're all winners says the nurse can you do me up I ask
you know the ropes better than anybody....

I can smell the knots she says

Sex is God and God is dead like that fuking mutt alright
like I dead shoulder blade through my skull alright cause I
didn't know, ok? It wasn't my fault, ok?

Moron.

Instant dead, instant but not if you slow it down scene by scene
through his last moments, last minutes, hours, days, years,
entire existence, all fusion at one moment, together again at
last, a reunion of the family, at last....

Let us try to <u>understand</u> a mass-murderer.

My step-mother phoned me and felt terribly sorry for the
families. I believe her. She'd been to a funeral at the Danish
Lutheran Church. One of her friends had died of cancer who
shouldn't have bothered with all the desperate and painful
attempts - chemo, lasers, etc. – *shouldn't have bothered;* don't
enjoy that concept very much; I understand why her friend did
it, why she scraped the last light from the bowl with her bleed-
ing claws; I hate existence but despise death.

Meanwhile, I indulge my pathos while others skate on it.

Alienation is interesting in my part of town; it smells like piña
colada concentrate, a sugary odour, tasty as coke on a casket.

Outside my window, two legs of traffic stream down the road,
deisel fumes blowing out of their dirty pipes, 70ft double-
container trucks clanking over an emerging hump, taxi after

taxi, groaning city buses and cop cars. Every sub-artic dawn the hump comes back through the pavement; it expands, contracts with the cold, and the traffic. It's like the back of some zombie who never quite sits up, approaching existence but retreating, encrusted by an inch of tar in the summer, some patching; that's alright, one year the grave will open....

White gas and piña colada hung over the neighbourhood, along St. Antoine, a noisy stunk afternoon and even the wettest dog shit freezes in four and a half minutes. The mute kid outside the depanneur told me that.

You learn a lot in my part of town. For instance, Mondays at 11AM the *Imperial Tobacco* factory down the street releases its menthol; it sticks on your clothes. Can't play ball-hockey with that stench, makes you cough, scratches the delicate lining of the lungs.

They put sugar in their cigarettes, glycerin in toothpaste, shit in my bath.

Yesterday, the cops raided my sister's boyfriend's apartment building and took Lester. They dumped his body at the back of *La Roi de Frankfurters* at the Anjou Mall in the east end. They say he was a drug dealer so I guess he had it coming, although he owed me twelve bucks.

As the cops would say – they have a difficult job to do and they're not perfect, just ask the families of Barnabe, Anthony Griffin, the guy they ambushed near Place Victoria.

I know who ratted on him. It was Momma, Momma Shellborn. My aunt. She doesn't like blacks so she called up her nephew Dominique who is on the force and he took it from there. Shelley is really upset but they've given her a lot of sedatives and won't let her out of bed until she signs a document and has an operation. See, she's pregnant and Momma wants to abort Lester's baby because it'll embarrass the family. That's what she says but I liked Lester and used to play ball hockey in the school yard below Notre Dame, near Rose de Lima. He had a great shot, man.

He told me that it was alright to jerk off. Momma used to say that you got aids from it. He told me it was alright to suk it if that's what I wanted and that most Canadians were rascist.

I'm not talking to anyone about it. Got enough trouble breathing.

Got a job interview at *Imperial Tobbacco* on Thursday. Momma set it up.

They say that they're building a train to New York that will only take 3 hrs. I hope so. Tired of it. I want to see junkies and shooting galleries. I want to see boys with tracks and work in a black bath-house and suk cock all this life and the next until MICHAEL RETURNS IN A CHARIOT OF FIRE AND EYES OF LIGHT. I got a cousin who's a fag like me (father shut door; tears - floor, etc.) on Ave. C. He's a dancer at the Pyramid Club. Where is that? I don't know, I'll find it, I'll find it.

Don't look under the page - just my cock, like you.

I hate Momma. I hate this town. They say that "Montreal is dominated by a mountain." It's not a mountain; it's a fuking hump of a sick mutt, tongue hanging off Westmount with their mansions and white bourgeois doorbells and perfect fingers. I make cigarettes for these assholes. Actually, I drive them, to *distribution centres,* ok? and I hate rich people because they have car-telephones and dress like chimps, most of them. I fuked this old Westmount guy but he was ok and gave me books instead of money and I have books. Hard to believe isn't it? I see that line of incredulity. Nice word, yr face is a nice page of lousy thin paper and I can read lines and do lines and I want to take that line outta here in 3 hrs.

I know this guy at *The New Yorker,* 841 Broadway. Said he'd hire me to clean his apartment with my tongue. I want to write for him, I want to write for the *Journal of International Relations* like Henry Kissinger and Dean Rusk.

I suked Lester after ball-hockey, dead man, fuk you fukers; not luv, not luv, just old mattresses, wasn't gigantic – *his humungus*

72

Negroid member finally pressed through Tony's thin pink hole, expanding it beyond human comprehension - ha ha ha, just giving me a break, uh, before the frogs beat my head in with their *Victoriaville* hockey sticks – *putain, putain, putain.*

It's a good life if yr dead.

I got a knife. I carry it in my shoes. I carry a smile and a knife.

I should have saved that dog. Or stabbed it but I don know where it is, probably with Lester in Hollywood. (Lester called anything that felt good "Hollywood" but he'd never been there either although he said it probably was full of shit too, like a lot of things....)

I'm not going to a party next wk at Momma's and I should stab her for what she does but I won't because it's too late and I don't believe in the myth of justice and because I don't believe in much anymore I can do things that people who do can't. And I am ahead of my time – I have to be otherwise I wouldn't have any money and have to keep that job at *Imperial Tobacco* and work with the rest of the jerks until MICHAEL BURNS IT ALL DOWN, until I get my pension and drink copious amounts of lousy *Labatt's*, until I die of liver exhaustion. Or aids because I'm so horny I take cock anywhere anytime— that's why I want to go to New York; to further my career.

I shaved off my hair for you and wait for you. I don't laugh anymore when the frogs tell me they'll tie wire around my wrists and dump me in the canal where all the dogs go. You should see all the dogs. They throw them on the ice and they fall under the locks and get mangled or drown in the rapids. I saw a dog's face looking up at me once; playing hockey and through the *glace* see this bloated green face and moonstone eyes, paw split, over his ear flap. Dead? Course, he's fuking dead, they don't float so the cops don't care, no one cares if you don't float.

That's why Lester is such a pain thing, you know? They dumped his body where they knew *Le Journal* would find it and they did it as a public statement, an announcement that Blacks Couldn't Fuk Immaculate White Girls. Of course, if I was raped by a platoon of *Canadiens,* they'd let it blow. So I *know* now what he was talking about and why he smiled and pulled it out for me, sayin – "have a good time, my man."

Where's the fukin' nurse; I want to die tonight. Lie down on somebody and die, die, die.

I see fuking squirrels, right? Hoppin' over puddles of slush and ice, under cars and scurrying up leafless grey trees as hard as bone, blizzard dust – and don't get it; why I feel so fuked and why this street is so fuked and I want to rescue Shelley and cut Momma, bury acorns in her putrid eyes for squirrels to dig out with sharp claws and watch tv and get her guts blown away like Lee Harvey Oswald and watch tv and find out why I feel so fuked and watch tv.

Henn

you lie on the cold lawn
feel sick
sky rushes
up yr neck
floods the warehouse

you talk about it so much
no one is really surprised

this smiling summer

the cold lawn
ices up as you greet him
and vomit

greet him and vomit
this is the way
you deal with dignity
this is the first, the precious jewel
taken from yr sleeve
  yr fuking beret, yr black pupils, yr social
  liver, yr soft white skin; waxy, still, pale,
  so young
  yr smile thin and laconic, this silly age
    you laugh — this *timelessness* —
      words,   words,   words
        dick,   dick,   dick

Did you haunt her until the last
Did you whisper

Who'll take you now
take you now on the tray
into the shadows of fire
broken tracks now

You greet him
You greet him
You greet him
  and vomit
  under the
  under under
  the skin
  whispers
no one listens
not even yrself
not even this romantic
ironic
  this ironic

I am the arsonist

I turn and leave and breathe you
and see and touch you and feel you
melt
into the centre softly.

Is there a mirror to remember you by
some phrase, a photo, a stash of poems
that you bled upon

  is it grief
  or ecstasy
   upon yr final blue tongue

Under the night sky
the black leaves
clap and cheer
along the boulevard
along the boulevard
another pulled from the gutter.

I sleep
   under you

the dog has started to drink.

Off the Decarie Expressway

the grey car falls towards paradise
and no one in the car
remembers where they were

The cow's head is leaking a putrid milky fluid. It is a warm September day and the traffic is so slow it seems that the occupants are in an American road video about the relativity of time and the inevitability of death which is odd since Bobby, the guitar player, driver and leader of the band has Hodgskin's disease and Dorothy, the singer and Bobby's girlfriend doesn't have a care in the world. She will miraculously survive the unfortunate occurences of existence to find happiness in rocks, swap meets and old phrases. Two years hence, at the age of twenty-four, Bobby will die in agony with surgeons pocketing through his kidneys for caviar and disease before his heart will give it up, take a walk, all fall down.

Meanwhile the cow's head they bought in St. Abbatoir is leaking through the plastic garbage bag into the Honda's upholstery. Since Bobby borrowed the car from Erik's mom she will be coughing for months because she's allergic to animal fluids. But Bobby believes it's Art; he'll have stuck a pole into the head and waved it around during one of his band's gigs, this time in a Laval Cegep and the effort will have been worth it because it's always important to make an impact. His band was known as the dirtiest, darkest, most aggressive band in Montreal.

Dorothy stuck her fingers between his legs wiggled them under his shorts and felt Bobby's genitals. The cock was long and soft in the heat. She pulled it and got it a little hard before pulling it out from under the underwear into the daylight. She looked at the fat pink head poking out of the loose foreskin pulled it back and over and then dived into his crotch, taking it deep as the traffic slowed and Bobby turned up the radio.

In the sky the clouds were orange and herded into pens like sheep before the sharp horizon.

Bobby was thinking about his guitar as usual as he shot over her fingers. "I should get new strings and then the whole fucking box reharnessed" he said to himself as he smiled at Dorothy. She wiped her lips and put his drooling meat back in the garage. She thought she was a naughty girl because she gave head in the Honda but it wasn't Bobby's first time. Yesterday, Erik the drummer had fuked him over the trunk. Bobby enjoyed that more especially because he hated Erik and would like to fire him for missing the beat all the time except he was rich.

It is ironic to think that Bobby was already dying, tiny cancers eating his lymph glands as he drove Erik's grey car up the Laurentien Autoroute towards this idiot gig at a Cegep the cow's brown pulpy lips saying "I love you, moo" as the two hundred kids in the hall jumped around and said it was alright, man.

Erik pounded out the beat to the wrong song but it didn't matter. The sound system scratched Bobby's voice and the guitars clichéd in the wrong key at max volume. Ken and Sailor did the hair-show, the kids deaf, stoned out, shaking to beautiful Erik, half-naked, thin willowy chest, face obliterated by hair, just the plump bright lower lip shaking, pounding the drums with the total dedication of youthful fanaticism. Dorothy stood stoic-like holding her bass; wrecked; black halter top, bondaged tits smiling under Bobby's plaid vest trying to cope with Erik's trip, all over the fuking map.

They had done it perfectly during the sound-check.

Centre-stage, Bobby sung about Morocco, buying hash from the bright kaftan man near the cenotaph. The guy had ripped him but not outrageously. Bobby felt alright, on the terrace like this with the freighters in the bay and a large chunk under his dresser.

He improvised in phrases, AB AB CD, repeated the chorus, break, solo, AB AB CD CD and out. Somehow it worked.

Dorothy was with him in Morocco, downstairs at this moment instructing the bartender on the theory of Manhattens, Martinis and Margueritas. She always had to do this; instruct the bartenders in every new hotel so she wouldn't get poisoned. She wore bangles and leather, she was plump in her period, he latex pants bulging at the waist. She smelt, changed her tampon in the taxi on the way from the airport, Bobby almost heaved. "Smoke it" she said and held the bloody thing in front of his face.

Two days later he changed hotels, left her behind, all she did was complain and talk about nothing; she was highly rated, good at flattery and maternal gestures. In fact. she was a heartless bitch who'd sell her kid sister for a nickle.

Meanwhile the grey car flips off the overpass and Erik's floating body awaits a crushing experience, black flags wave over Beaconsfield, let's get dead, Erik.

Erik shouldn't have drove, no matter how tired everybody else got....

Where's Sammy, the producer from Chicago who lifts weights, takes you home and comes on even if you hate him. He plays fireman and he has the gear, boots, axe, helmet. And coke. He likes to pull drunk straight guys from the bars on Crescent St; he doesn't care about death and he'll die, he'll die for you, he says, for the sake of any story you want....

If I could remember them all, the faces flipping like cards in a shark's movie, all the dead and the young ones, and the survivors aging into sobriety and thick chests and faces, wives and babies, jobs; cheerful now and older, with less promises and bitterness than expected, clouds of blood rising through the sky attracting others and more and many....

Yes, Erik died although it was ok because his father had no money left anyway and he would have been a very ugly junkie so that's better, isn't it dear? Cup of Tea?

Ah, Bobby, this is a story about Bobby who was a lot cooler than me, I am conservative, quieter. I watched him. I could see some of what was happening but it's him carrying the charisma, a cigarette between the corners of his lips in the dressing room before that last gig, looking wretched but wiser, back, stuck with Dorothy like glue knowing she hated me for loving him even though the fuking we did was boring and she had no reason to be jealous; I just wanted to taste it that's all.

She had a dirty mouth so it was wiser to let her go on a bit, especially if she was doing coke which she'd been doing since time began to control her weight.

Bobby's parents came to the funeral by bus but I gave them taxi fare home. He hadn't told them that Paris was a great city but Montreal was great enough 'cause his parents were stupid and holy and he couldn't stand their knick-knacks.

Some towns you don't go back to.

I don't know why Bobby authorized the fuking exploratory surgery, fuking nuts, the pain was insane, tearing his face.

I don't see Dorothy much anymore. That scene is dead anyway. I guess, she's around here somewhere. There's enough bars.

Funny thing, she expected to get some money but Bobby left it to an animal shelter in Ste. Agathe, he knew what a fuk she really was.

Will we be small-time forever
the mascara host
the suk-ass telephone conversationalist
asking about trips to the sun
to New York
hearing the beginning of every story
nodding in the corner of some slow cocktail flesh
the hero of a small party
glint of the addict's eye
beauty's spore
the tongue licking piss from the walls
where you scrape yr name
some name some thought
in the effort of forever
a comic of suicide

no sense of humour obviously
no sense of it all
of it all

Where is the big time, the night of the
grand ball, the podium, the altar, the climax
when the priest blows incense and starlets kiss the awards
the Aztecs used to cut my heart from my chest
many times
I've starred in the Joy Division
redecorated the walls of motel rooms off the
interstate with the cheap wallpaper cheap cheap cheap
lives
my lives
we will die
again

Do you want a colour tv?

thin blood spits into a radiant pool from the nostrils
around the man of steel I step over him and piss a long time,
he's pawing me, feel his fingers near my boots

everybody loves me
I am a busboy

It's late, I start taking apart the umbrellas on the terrace
heaving the weighted bases along the wet floor towards the
storeroom

I have a room on Mozart
some nights I sleep on the fire-escape

I remember Manitoba
big sky land you could see the weather a hundred miles away

I still miss him, always will, his face, his eyes. his lips giving me
tattoes and smokey, stunk, dirty kisses between the stories,
dreams, fuks. . . .

Where will it end, I don't know what I'll do. I don't know.

I'm asymptomatic right now; a beauty queen

I may fall or, you know, I may not.

Exactly, exactly.

Do you want a colour tv?

I got wings
a beak
claws
lesions.

I don't have much time.

I live under the eaves
of a tenement.

I watch you

sip wine in the police car —

you're terrific,

every step, every moment.

I got yr list, the things you missed

the promotion
the sex
the mortgage
the respect of yr peers
what else
blah, blah, blah.

The streets are crazy
the music's overproof.
Who cares about guitars,

who cares ?

In North Carolina I rip a kiss
from the gas-attendant
suk the soda-jerk
in the can,

Sarah Lee in the pick-up,

piss on a jerk with a rep
drink the kiss from the teenager with an ax
my brains hung out of my head.

I demand drugs and some cash
and a son in *Scouts.*

Did you see the sunset?
It happens everyday but this one was special

sure
a cure

a nurse falling from a hearse.

This is my will—
spray my dust
like a tom-cat

between a boulder split like a skull
on a Saturday night

totally pissed

break a sullen
moth-like pause

with pumping-cock reverence I sigh

in memory for
those who hold the torch.

I haunt bowling alleys
painted in industrial flames

I drop my skin like a wet towel

O *Ham*let

On summer nights
hustlers
kiss each other
until they're fuking
and losing it.

All this polite grieving folds into nothing.

too many things
too much

happening
only the days are the same

the sun so short

regrets too profound
and inevitable

where are the bells
in the machine
like everything else

what about the show
what about the movies

nobody knows what I'm talking about
it's raining tv's
and Donna Reed
and romantic dinners in Florida

singing cops
pull each other in the ruins of the warehouse

23/12/91

under the bridge
I share the glue
with the dogs

the way I walk
the spore growing off my shoulder
knuckle on my neck

I knew it was over

I live but my
sperm is weak and yellow

staggering dogs watch the water
revolt and boil

flashes of hope

a sparkle of aluminum foil
in the long darkness

a wet tongue covered with lesions

25/12/91

slap the cream
into the wound
watch the virus
grow
watch the ulcers
multiply
watch the rats
scurry
madly in the case

hang the starving dogs
from their hind-legs
on a scaffold next to
the victim likewise hung

watch the eyes of the mob
caress the scene

listen to the voice
whispering
as the guts spill
to the boiling floor

25/12/91

In the mute night
cold streets

broken by the scream of a
cat or a lover

strung to a glorious wire
or numb to an itch

long lines dressed in maroon
handing chocolate beards
to no one at all

where is this dance I heard about
where is this man who takes you now

stuck in love

jealousy compounds my grief

there's someone to see you
they tell me
leaning in a suit against the wall

says he's heard about it
brought a leash

says he's been waiting
he'll come back soon

All the trees have lost their hair
All the stories broke like beggars
All the veins cut into ribbons
painted limbs float through space

the earth is free

24/12/93

As the disease barks
through the curtain

As dogs sink

As lights fall

As dark rivers whisper
below the dressing-gown

the rusty dawn screams
glory, glory

Ω   Ω   Ω

Snow cuts sideways across the tombs,
blowing the end off my cheap American cigarette
bare ankles eaten by frost
Come on, baby, come on
Where are you, where are you?

I kneel opposite a disciple with a burnt face
and chewed cuffs.
He says he's thinking about cracks.
I ask him if I can crawl in when we're swept away
in the hellstorm - he said he'd get back
to me on that

Glory, glory
glory, glory

all the time

REPORT ON THE 2ND HALF OF THE TWENTIETH CENTURY
BK. 8-11
KEN NORRIS

IN THE SPIRIT OF THE TIMES
KEN NORRIS

SYMPHONY
ELIAS LETELIER-RUZ
Tr. Ken Norris

SILENCE
ELIAS LETELIER-RUZ
Tr. Ken Norris

NA VRAITH ZVECER/AT THE DOOR AT EVENING
EDVARD KOCBECK
Tr. Tom Lozar
John Glassco Translation Prize Nominee

INTERIOR DESIGNS
ROBIN POTTER

HOW TO
ENDRE FARKAS
A.M. Klein Poetry Prize Nominee '88

THE OTHER LANGUAGE
ED. ENDRE FARKAS
Montreal Perfect Library Prize Nominee '90?

DYING WITH AIDS/LIVING WITH AIDS
MARK LESLIE

THE COST OF LIVING
KENNETH RADU
Governor General Award Nominee

THE MUSES' COMPANY

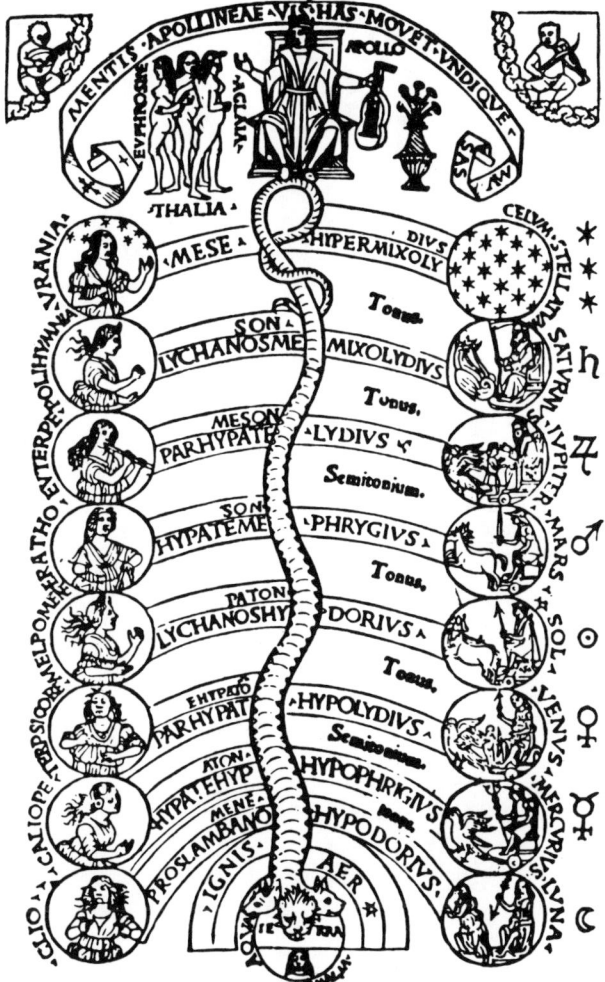

LA COMPAGNIE DES MUSES